Stress Busting for Musicians

Irene Lock

Illustrations by Drew Hillier

And with a preface by
Wayne Topping, PhD.

First published in 2006 by Queen's Temple Publications
Printed in Scotland by Spartan Press.

Copyright © 2006 by Queen's Temple Publications

Queen's Temple Publications
15 Mallard Drive
Buckingham
MK18 1GJ

Distributed by Spartan Press
Strathmashie House
Laggan Bridge
Scottish Highlands
PH20 1BU

Foreword

The act of performing or playing music is highly involved and the potential for stress and tension is immense. Simply operating a musical instrument or singing is itself a multifaceted and complex activity, where we often ask our bodies to contort or work in unnatural ways. Additionally our minds have to be clear to allow a full range of artistic, musical and interpretive thoughts. And on top of that there are the pressures and anxieties of public performance, competitions, auditions or exams.

Whatever kind of musician you are, this book will help deal with and control all those possible tensions and dissipate stress. Only then can we really give of our best – and, what's more, we can really begin to enjoy the experience!

Irene Lock has provided a series of simple and practical exercises based on her wide experience and training, designed especially for musicians to release their potential and experience a stress-free physical and emotional environment in which to thrive.

Paul Harris

Preface

I remember being very surprised many years ago when I read of research showing that approximately 26% of the musicians surveyed were on tranquilizers. I naively assumed that because they were outwardly calm and were clearly competent that they must be enjoying their performing. I have since come to recognise that outward appearance and internal physiology can be quite different.

Each of us carries a library of our past experiences, oftentimes including upsetting or even traumatic experiences from schooling or early performances. Sadly, for far too many of us, these unresolved issues of the past interfere with our ability to perform up to our full potential in the present.

Fortunately, we now have numerous simple, fast and effective tools to defuse that stress. Professional musicians will be able to break free from those past traumas. Parents and music teachers will have the tools to help their children and students minimize the stresses that accompany learning and performing and to increase their enjoyment and creativity.

Many of my colleagues and I changed careers once we became exposed to the type of exercises Irene has described here. We have been excited by the changes they bring about within the individuals we work with and we are sharing them as effectively as we can.

I was very pleased to introduce Irene to some of these techniques and I am very happy that she has chosen to share them with those of you in the music world. Have fun and may you benefit greatly from these stress busters.

Wayne Topping, PhD.
Founder, Wellness Kinesiology.
Author of "Success Over Distress"

Introduction

This book is the result of a long journey back to health from M.E. or Chronic Fatigue Syndrome. At the start of my journey I was physically unable to stand and play or to teach without my body letting me down in some way, due to the stress and tension these activities caused me. My hands would shake uncontrollably, my legs would feel they did not belong to me and my breath control and technique were at the least unreliable, at the worst, nonexistent. I seemed to be sapped of all of my energies. An impossible situation for a clarinet player and woodwind teacher. I have learnt during my journey back to health that when stressed the brain stops working in the most efficient way, we have to use different strategies to access our learning, making it more stressful and at the same time some muscles actually switch off. This causes other muscles to do the opposite and overreact, working overtime leading to changes in posture. The body's balances are upset and the symptoms of stress kick in; tension in muscles leads to aches and pains, sweating, shaking, dry mouth, lack of concentration, memory loss, to name just a few. Also I was starving my mind of the necessary 'food' it needed to work efficiently. All of this led to a breakdown in the system allowing viruses to run rampant, which I found more and more difficult to recover from.

I have learnt that by simply giving my brain and body the help it needs to work effectively, through the use of the exercises in this book, I can perform and work at an intensity which lets my body get on with the job without draining it of all of its resources. I hope this book will help you to do the same. It will help you to put all of your energies into making and enjoying music whatever instrument you play; it will enable you to work at your optimum level.

I would like to thank the following people for believing in me and encouraging me back to health, my husband Brian, without whose support none of this would have been possible. Mark Church, my kinesiologist who showed me what was happening to my body, introduced me to kinesiology and taught me how to make some of the changes I needed. Roland Mann and Robin Wells, both kinesiologists and musicians who gave me further insight as to what was happening to my body. Wayne Topping who changed my life completely by showing me both how serious an effect stress can have and how I could defuse it. Peter Nichols, David Campbell, Victoria Soames Samek and Angela Malsbury, the clarinettists who helped to keep me playing and teaching. All of my pupils, both adult and youngsters, who have shown me how much this book is needed and who acted as case studies to try out the exercises, and finally Paul Harris, my teacher, friend and mentor, who suggested I write this book and has supported me throughout the process.

Section 1

Pre-practice Warm Ups and Energizers

Do the following exercises before starting any learning or playing. They will switch your brain and body on with maximum efficiency and minimum effort. The work will feel smoother and you will retain the knowledge more easily.

Exercises Essential to Warming Up

1 Drink Plain Water

To enable your brain to work at its optimum level it needs a regular supply of plain water.

1.1 As you drink, the receptors in the sides of your mouth immediately send a message to the brain to release some of the water stored in the cells from all parts of your body; what you have just swallowed is then used to replace the stored water. Your brain needs the water to help form the electrical circuits, which fuels the neural pathways or message senders in your brain. The water must be plain - tap, mineral, spring or filtered are all acceptable - as the body sees any flavouring e.g. fruit juice, squash, tea, coffee, alcohol, etc. as a food. A glass of water will simply cause your brain to work better!

2 Switch on your Electrical Circuits

This is done to make sure your brain can communicate clearly with the rest of your body. It gets rid of any cross messaging between the two hemispheres of the brain and makes sure the messages reach all parts of the body, preventing blockages which may occur during times of stress.

There are four exercises to do. Notice how you feel after each one.

2.1 Find your collarbone or clavicle. Start by hunching your shoulders forward and feel the bone, which is across your chest, just below the shoulders and in front of your neck. This is easily done over your clothing. When you have found the bone relax your shoulders back. There are two knobs on this bone, towards the middle of your chest, which are the bone-ends. Place the thumb of one hand on one knob and your index and middle finger of the same hand on the other knob. Move your fingers down to about 1 cm. below the knobs, to where the skin dips in slightly. You are going to massage these dips, with your thumb, index and middle fingers. To stabilise and to complete the circuit place the other hand over your navel (or tummy button) and keep it still. Give the dips a good massage for approximately 20-30 seconds and then swap your hands over. The dips are acupuncture point 27 on the kidney meridian, for those who like the science! If the dips are painful, ease off the pressure and massage for longer. This massage switches on and co-ordinates the left and right sides of the body. It also helps to clear the mind, essential when starting to practice or play music. This exercise is very good to wake up the system if you are feeling slightly under par. (N.B. If you are an epileptic do each of the dips separately, first one side with the other hand over the navel, then change sides.)

How do you feel? Do you notice any changes to your eyesight or hearing?

2.2 Next place your thumb pad just below your bottom lip and the index and middle finger pads just above your top lip; these are the next massage spots. Make sure you are using the finger pads, digging your nails in is painful. Again place the other hand over your navel to stabilise and to complete the circuit. Give the spots a good massage for approximately 20-30 seconds and then change hands. You are stimulating one end of the central and governing meridians, which will improve your concentration and help you to take in new knowledge. This also switches on the connection between the top and bottom of your body. This will also help with reading notation and, if you're playing or singing in a group, an orchestra or band, it will help with the movement of your eyes from your music to the conductor and back again.

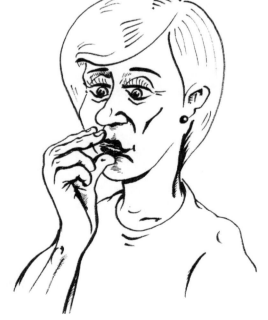

How do you feel?

2.3 Leave one hand on your navel and place the other on your tailbone. Give this a good massage, for 20-30 seconds and then change hands. This co-ordinates or switches on the back and front of the body making you aware of your spine as well as what the front of your body is doing. This is the other end of the governing meridian, which allows us to accept changes and move on from the past i.e. improve on how we do things. This will also help with reading music notation.

How do you feel?

2.4 The final exercise will also help to improve your concentration and motivation. This is stimulating the energy pathway to the brain or central meridian, which helps us to make changes easily, i.e. take in new learning. Imagine you are wearing a long jacket, which has a zip from the top of your legs to just below your bottom lip going up the midline of your body. Zip the jacket up, several times, taking your hands down away from your body. Another way of visualising this is to picture some water, which you scoop up in one hand and then the other to wash your lower face. It is very important that you do not go higher than your bottom lip or you may feel confused and lose concentration, rather than improve it.

Notice how you feel.

Don't forget to keep drinking some water during your practice to top up the circuits.

3 Coordinating Left and Right

This exercise improves further the left and right co-ordination of your brain. It helps with aural work, visual reading of a musical score, and being able to work equally on both left and right hand sides of the body.

3.1 Lift and bend the right knee and touch it with the left hand *over the midline of your body*. Keep your knee straight in front of you. Repeat using the left knee and right hand. Make sure you cross over to meet at the midline of your body. Do this at an Adagio not an Allegro. For a change you can also do this behind your body, using the opposite hand and foot. If you are sitting down, you can lift the right foot and at the same time touch the right knee with the left hand, then do the same with the left foot and knee with right hand, making sure you cross the midline of your body with your arms. This needs to be repeated about 20 times.

8

Some people find this exercise very difficult and are unable to co-ordinate the opposite hand and knee. If this is the case, first try lifting the same arm and leg like a puppet on a string. Do this at *Grave*, up, down, stop, think with the right side; then up, down, stop, think on the left side. Repeat about 10 times. Now try the first exercise, crossing over your body at the midline. It will become easier with time and patience. This exercise is one your body really needs to help it work really effectively. It co-ordinates both sides of the brain, improves concentration, makes taking in new learning easier, helps general co-ordination, focus and energy.

Section 2

Exercises to help physically relax your body for playing

Exercises to be added for a 5-10 minute warm-up.
This set of exercises will help develop a relaxed and balanced posture.

4 Standing

Start by standing as you would do normally. How does your body feel? Does it feel equal on both sides? Does one shoulder feel higher than the other? Does one leg feel longer or shorter than the other? Are both arms the same length? Is your neck relaxed? Is your throat relaxed? Is you head sitting lightly on top of you spine? Is your head centrally balanced or pointing up, down, forward of centre or backwards?

Choose one or more of the following (as required).

5 Feet and Legs

5.1 Stand with your feet shoulder width apart and your feet parallel. Relax your legs and bounce on your knees a couple of times to check that they are not locked. Move your feet and toes inside your shoes to check that your weight is evenly spread between both feet. Tension even in your little toe can affect your playing. If you are standing for any length of time keep checking that your knees don't lock by occasionally doing a little bounce. This keeps your posture relaxed and without tension, which will allow you to concentrate on your music.

6 Whole Body Alignment

6.1 Now imagine a string, attached to the top of your head, and held by a puppeteer above you. Let the puppeteer gently pull the string upwards and notice how your head position alters. You are now letting your head sit at the top of your spine. This release of the tension in your throat and neck allows the air to travel in and out of your body unimpeded. You may also feel taller, and clearer in the mind.

7 Shoulders

7.1 Firstly imagine you are carrying two equally heavy bags of shopping one in each hand. Now feel how both arms hang loosely from your shoulders. Now write your name in the air with each of your shoulders; moving just your shoulder, not the arm. This relaxes all of the shoulder, upper chest and back muscles. You will now feel more relaxed; releasing tension here will have an effect all over your body. Use this exercise when things are not going well in practice or when you can feel the tension impeding finger control.

8 Arms 1

8.1 Take note of where the tips of your fingers are, as your arms hang, relaxed by your sides. Now lift one arm as if shaking a friend's hand, but imagining they are further away from you than you think, stretch your arm out to take hold of theirs, keep your body still and straight. Feel the stretch down the side of

your body into your ribs, and then relax your arm back down the side of your body. Note where your fingers reach on the side of your body: you have lengthened the muscles allowing them to relax, releasing tension and stress. Now repeat with the other arm. Relaxed muscles in your arms allow faster and more nimble finger work and a relaxed neck/throat area.

9 Arms 2

9.1 You are now going to conduct with both hands mirroring each other. Start this at a *Largo*. Keep your eyes looking ahead and level. Try different time signatures and gestures; use small and large ones. Now move on to *Adagio*, *Moderato* and *Allegro* speeds. Make sure your hands mirror each other and are in front of the middle of your body. This will help with left and right co-ordination.

10 Hands 1

10.1 Give your hands a good rub, move the skin over your bones. Imagine you are a surgeon scrubbing up for an operation. This will get the blood moving, and if they are cold it will warm them up – much healthier than immersing them in hot water.

11 Hands 2

11.1 Place one hand on to a flat solid surface. Spread out your fingers and thumb in a fan shape. Keeping the main area of your hand flat on the surface, lift each finger in turn and tap a bar of four crotchets or quarter notes, without moving the other fingers. This gives each finger a good stretch relieving the tension. It will become easier with practice and each finger will be able to give a strong tap, independently of the others.

Don't forget to **keep** drinking some **water** during your practice to top up the circuits.

Section 3

Exercises for Further Improving your Concentration, Memory and Eyes.

12 Ears

12.1 You are going to *unfold* each ear. Start at the top of your ear, close to your head; use two fingers to support behind the ear and your thumb on top to gently unfold your ears. This can be done one at a time or both together. When you reach the lobe, place your thumb underneath it to give support and give a gentle tug all along it. Repeat this three times with each ear. This helps to improve hearing, memory, vision and breathing. In the ears there are over 400 reflex points, which represent a map of the body (similar to reflexology and the feet.) This

exercise stimulates them. Violin, viola and flute players can add turning the head to the left whilst unfolding the left ear and then to the right whilst unfolding the right ear, which will help to release the tension caused by holding the head at an unnatural angle while playing. Repeat the unfolding three times with each ear.

13 Eyes 1

13.1 When your eyes start to feel tired after reading lots of music, or you have to read poorly written manuscript, first repeat Exercise 2.1, massaging the dips below the collarbones with the other hand on the navel. At the same time as you do this, turn your head and eyes first to the left, then to the right, followed by just moving your eyes left and right, up and down, taking your eyes as far as you can in each direction. Finish with tracking your eyes across from side to side as far as they will go. This will improve your music reading skills and your understanding of the music. If you wear glasses, try doing this without them, to help improve your eyesight.

14 Eyes 2

14.1 If you wear glasses, remove them. Take your hands and rub them together vigorously to create some heat. Place a warm hand over each of your eyes and absorb the warmth, looking at the darkness created. This will refresh your eyes to continue reading music.

15 Jaw release

15.1 Open your mouth and pretend to give a big yawn; this improves your vision and makes you feel more alert with the change to fresh oxygen. If you also massage your cheeks where the jaws join, at the same time as you open your mouth to yawn, this will improve your ability to read music and thinking will be clearer. You will be able to cut out any background distracting noises and your facial muscles will also relax. You are massaging the temporomandibular joint through which passes many of the nerves which supply the head.

16 Deep Breathing

16.1 This is something "blowing" and singing musicians should do automatically, but how many do? Place your hands on your waist, take in a big breath, your hands should move outwards as the lungs expand and the diaphragm moves downwards. Do not move your shoulders upwards (this is "chest breathing" which inhibits the correct use of the diaphragm.) Another way in which you can feel this deep breathing is to lie on the floor, on your back, with your knees raised to support the lower back. Place a small instrument case or large book on to your stomach and watch it rise as you breathe in, and lower as you breathe out. If you cannot lie on the floor, imagine you are wearing a skirt or trousers with a very loose waistband and no belt. Push out with your abdominal muscles to keep the garment from falling down.

When you can control this technique, inhale deeply over a count of 4; hold your breath for 4, and breathe out for 4. Gradually decrease the time you take to breathe in and increase the holding and breathing out time. This will increase the oxygen in your blood, providing you with more energy, making you feel more wide-awake for better concentration and increasing your lung capacity.

Don't forget to **keep** drinking some **water** during your practice to top up the circuits.

Section 4

Dealing with Stress in Performance, Examinations or Auditions

There are two types of stress: eustress and distress. Eustress is the positive; how a child feels when anticipating a birthday or Christmas for example. Distress is the musicians' biggest enemy. It can seriously affect our love of and ability to perform music, our very lifeblood. This is when stress becomes negative and rules our thinking and actions. These exercises are in three cumulative parts. They will help you to deal in a positive way with any stressful situation be it past, present or future. They can be done well in advance or just before a performance, examination or audition. They can also be done during a concert interval or afterwards to de-stress the situation. Many musicians have been down the beta-blocker or alcohol route to conquer nerves or stress. Unfortunately this only buries the symptoms, storing up more stress for the future. Remember what it feels like when things don't go well and then having to play the same thing on another occasion be it piece, scale or exercise? These stressful memories become a reflex action and we do not use the front, thinking part of our brains, but instead we rely on the automatic reactive thinking from the more primitive parts of our brains. The following exercises turn this remembered stress into a memory, which the body can file away, allowing it to concentrate on the new performance, examination or audition, by using our conscious mind.

If the stress you are dealing with is particularly traumatic, start by setting up a "safe place," real or imaginary, where you feel happy and stress free. Go to the safe place as often as you feel necessary, to take time out from the following process.

17.1 Emotional Stress Release Points

These points are on your forehead, where we would have had horns. Your forehead has a slight bump or eminence at this spot, directly above your eyes and midway between your eyebrows and hairline. Place the index and middle finger of each hand on each of these points. This brings you back into the thinking, reasoning front part of your brain, away from the fight or flight instinct part, which is where we go when we are stressed. Use a very light pressure, as if you were touching your eyeball.

Think about your stressful situation. Give the stressful feeling a score out of ten. Zero being no stress and ten being maximum stress. Keep thinking about the stressful situation; gradually the score will go down. If the score reaches zero, or your mind starts to wander you have successfully turned the stress into a memory the brain can file safely away. If the score gets stuck continue with the next exercise, the eye rotations.

The Emotional Stress Release points are neurovascular holding points, which were discovered in the 1930s by Terrence Bennett, a chiropractor. Dr George Goodheart, also a chiropractor, did further work on them in the 1960s and 1970s. When we react negatively to stress, lots of chemical, emotional and physical changes happen very quickly in our bodies, known as the fight or flight syndrome. We are being controlled by reflex actions instead of our conscious minds. A red angry face or draining away of colour when we are scared are examples of these changes. Touching the Emotional Stress Release points allows us to send messages via the nervous system to the vascular or blood system, opening up the capillary networks to bring us back to our reasoning, thinking part of our brains. When we recall the situation in the future it will not take us into the reflex reaction. The past, present or future view of the stressful situation has changed.

15

17. 2 Eye Rotations

While keeping your fingers on the Emotional Stress Release Points, at a Largo, rotate your eyes in each direction, clockwise and anti-clockwise. If there is a place on the rotations where the eye muscles ache or feel uncomfortable keep your eyes in that spot until the ache eases, usually a few seconds. Complete the eye rotations stopping wherever the eyes feel uncomfortable. Again, if the score reaches zero or your mind starts to wander you have successfully turned the stress into a memory the brain can file away. If your score gets stuck, go on to the final exercise. Remember to use the "safe place" if you need to.

17.3 The Finger Modes

Gently place the pads of your thumb and ring (or fourth finger) together and keep them there while you return your index and middle fingers back on to the Emotional Stress Release points. At the same time repeat the eye rotations. Keep thinking about the stressful situation and note your score. Again aim for zero or your mind wandering. Remember to use the "safe place" if you need to. If your score is still not at zero repeat these exercises daily for up to three weeks. Doing them first thing in the morning before getting up and at night, just before sleeping will be a great help.

Remember you can do these exercises for a past, present or future stress. When you use them for a future stressful event visualise how you want the performance to go, put in as much positive detail as possible about the venue, audience, examiner or audition panel, even what you will be wearing. Your brain cannot tell the difference between a visualisation and a real event, so pre-programming it with positive thoughts will defuse any perceived stress. For a past stressful event, put in the fine details, this time concentrate on all the distress it caused you. This time the exercises will defuse the distress from your memories allowing you to move on and not become stuck with negative memories, which reappear when a similar situation occurs.

For a present stress also try using the exercises as described below for public places. These exercises will allow your body to turn any stress; real or perceived into a memory the brain can file away. You are reacting positively to the stress and moving on. It will no longer have an effect on your playing, learning or performance.

18 Calming down

18.1 This exercise is especially useful for calming you down before any performance and is in two parts. Part one: Whilst sitting place the left ankle over your right knee; hold the left ankle with your right hand and the bottom of your left foot with your left hand. If it is more comfortable you can do this the other way round, right ankle over left knee; hold the right ankle with your left hand and the bottom of your right foot with your right hand. Place your tongue, like a sheet along the roof of your mouth, keep your mouth shut and think about the breath going slowly in and out of your body, remain in this position for about 2 minutes, longer if you have time. Now let go of your ankle and foot. Part two: Place your fingertips together using very light pressure. Again keep still for about 2 minutes or longer. You may feel a 'fizz' between your fingertips, but don't worry if you can't.

Don't forget to **keep** drinking some **water** during your practice and while doing these exercises to top up the circuits. Water is a big stress buster.

Section 5

Using the Stress Exercises in Public

The previous stress exercises are best done in the privacy of our own homes or in the teaching studio, but sometimes we need to de-stress quickly, in an unobtrusive way, maybe during a concert or performance. Start with a drink of water, followed by the Emotional Stress Release Points and Calming Down as described below.

Cover the Emotional Stress Release Points by placing your whole hand over your forehead, use a very light pressure, again as if touching your eyeball. Another way is to use your thumb on one point and your index and middle finger on the other. This will quickly ease the stress - and no one will know what you are doing, this is a very natural pose you might adopt if you had a headache or were studying.

Do the Calming Down exercise without gripping the feet. Instead cross your ankles, checking to see you have done so in the most comfortable way, either right over left or left over right. Place your hands back to back in your lap, cross one hand over the other in the same way as your ankles i.e. right over left or left over right and intertwine your fingers. Place your tongue in the same way on to the roof of your mouth. Then place your fingertips together as before. This variation, called Hook Ups, is from Brain Gym®, developed by Dr Paul and Gail Denison.

Placing a hand over the forehead is excellent to remove the stress during examinations, pupils can still hold their instrument; the examiner does not know what is happening, so the candidate is not embarrassed in using the exercise. Use it, for example, while studying the sight-reading exercise. Remember, this technique brings the brain out of the fight/flight or limbic area where you cannot think rationally and allows you to use the front or reasoning part of the brain. It is therefore very useful when you have learnt something, but have a memory block, e.g. with scales, viva voce tests or before playing from memory.

Don't forget to **keep** drinking some **water;** this is the biggest aid to de-stressing.

Section 6

Mixing and Matching the Exercises

19 Learning a New Piece

The following group of exercises will speed up the learning process on a new piece. Begin by drinking some water, then the Switching On exercises (2.1 – 2.4) followed by Co-ordinating left and right (3.1). Include the Ears (12.1) here and add any other, which you consider particularly useful to you. Then while you **look** through the piece (without playing) hold the Emotional Stress Release Points (17.1 only). Do this before you play or sing a note to allow the learning process to be co-ordinated and make it a more enjoyable, easy, and flowing experience. You will also retain more fully the work you are about to do making for better progress.

20 Resurrecting an Old Piece for Performance

Start with some water, then hold the Emotional Stress Points (17.1 only) thinking about the last time you performed the piece. Put in as much detail as possible about the last performance, the venue, the audience, how you were feeling, how the performance went. Follow this with Calming Down (18.1) still thinking about the last performance. This removes the old stresses. Now do the Switching On exercises (2.1 – 2.4) followed by Co-ordinating left and right (3.1). Repeat the Emotional Stress Release Points while looking at the piece, then try any tricky technical passages prefacing each one with the Emotional Stress Release Points, visualising how you want each one to go before playing it. Finally play the piece through.

21 Learning a Piece from Memory

Again start with some water, Switching On (2.1 –2.4) followed by Co-ordinating left and right (3.1). Assuming you know the piece, use the Emotional Stress Release Points visualising the sort of performance you want from memory. Now do Ears (12.1) with your head straight. This combination will improve your retentive memory.

And Finally

These exercises are designed to enhance your musical life, to make it more of a pleasure whether practising at home or performing at any level. The preparatory exercises are an essential part of your warm up, as a preparation to smooth learning; those that deal with stress will help to defuse any anxiety and nervous tension. The remainder are to be used as necessary. You will find certain exercises seem to do more for you than others; we all have different needs and no two of us are quite alike. You will also find you develop your favourites, which seem to work for a range of problems. So…good luck with your playing and I wish you as stress-free a future as possible!

Bibliography and Further Reading

Dennison, Paul E. and Gail E "Brain Gym" Edu-Kinesthetics, Inc 1986
Hannaford, Carla, "The Dominance Factor", Great Ocean Publishers 1997
Hannaford, Carla, "Smart Moves", Great Ocean Publishers 1995
Harris, Paul, and Crozier, Richard, "The Music Teachers Companion", ABRSM 2000
MacDonald, Glynn, "The Complete Illustrated Guide to Alexander Technique", Element Books Ltd 1998
Promislow, Sharon "Making the Brain Body Connection" Kinetic Publishing Corporation 1999
Topping, Wayne, "Success over Distress", Topping International Institute 1990
Topping, Wayne, "Stress Release", Topping International Institute 1991